For Clio and Isla, my amazing doers.
Anyone seen the glue gun?
—Mom

To Eli, Naomi, and Alyse
on summer vacation
—Dad

Text copyright © 2017 by Dev Petty
Jacket art and interior illustrations copyright © 2017 by Mike Boldt

All rights reserved. Published in the United States by Doubleday, an imprint of Random House Children's Books,
a division of Penguin Random House LLC, New York.

Doubleday and the colophon are registered trademarks of Penguin Random House LLC.

Visit us on the Web! randomhousekids.com

Educators and librarians, for a variety of teaching tools, visit us at RHTeachersLibrarians.com

Library of Congress Cataloging-in-Publication Data is available upon request.

ISBN 978-0-399-55803-0 (trade) — ISBN 978-0-399-55804-7 (lib. bdg.) — ISBN 978-0-399-55805-4 (ebook)

MANUFACTURED IN CHINA
10 9 8 7 6 5 4 3 2 1
First Edition

Random House Children's Books supports the First Amendment and celebrates the right to read.

THERE'S NOTHING TO DO!

written by
Dev Petty

DOUBLEDAY BOOKS FOR YOUNG READERS

illustrated by
Mike Boldt

I can think of lots of things...
buuuuut I don't want to do any of them.

Rabbit, what should we do today?
Hop around in circles and then...

Owl, I don't know what to do. Do you have any ideas?
Sure. First find a nice spot.
And?
Sleep until it's dark....
And?
Wake up.
And?
That's it.
Who wants to spend the whole day sleeping?
I do. Good night.

Pig, I can't find anything to do.
Have you tried sniffing around in the dirt?
Why would I do that?
If you have to ask, I can't explain it to you.

Pig, I'm not sure this list qualifies as fantastic.
5. Wake Owl!
6. Spin around

What's the matter?
The day is almost over and I didn't do anything.

Why do you have to do anything? Just be. Watch clouds go by. Think about stuff. Then put **DO NOTHING** on your to-do list, and check it off. Sometimes the best ideas come when you stop looking for them.

Really?

Let's try it....

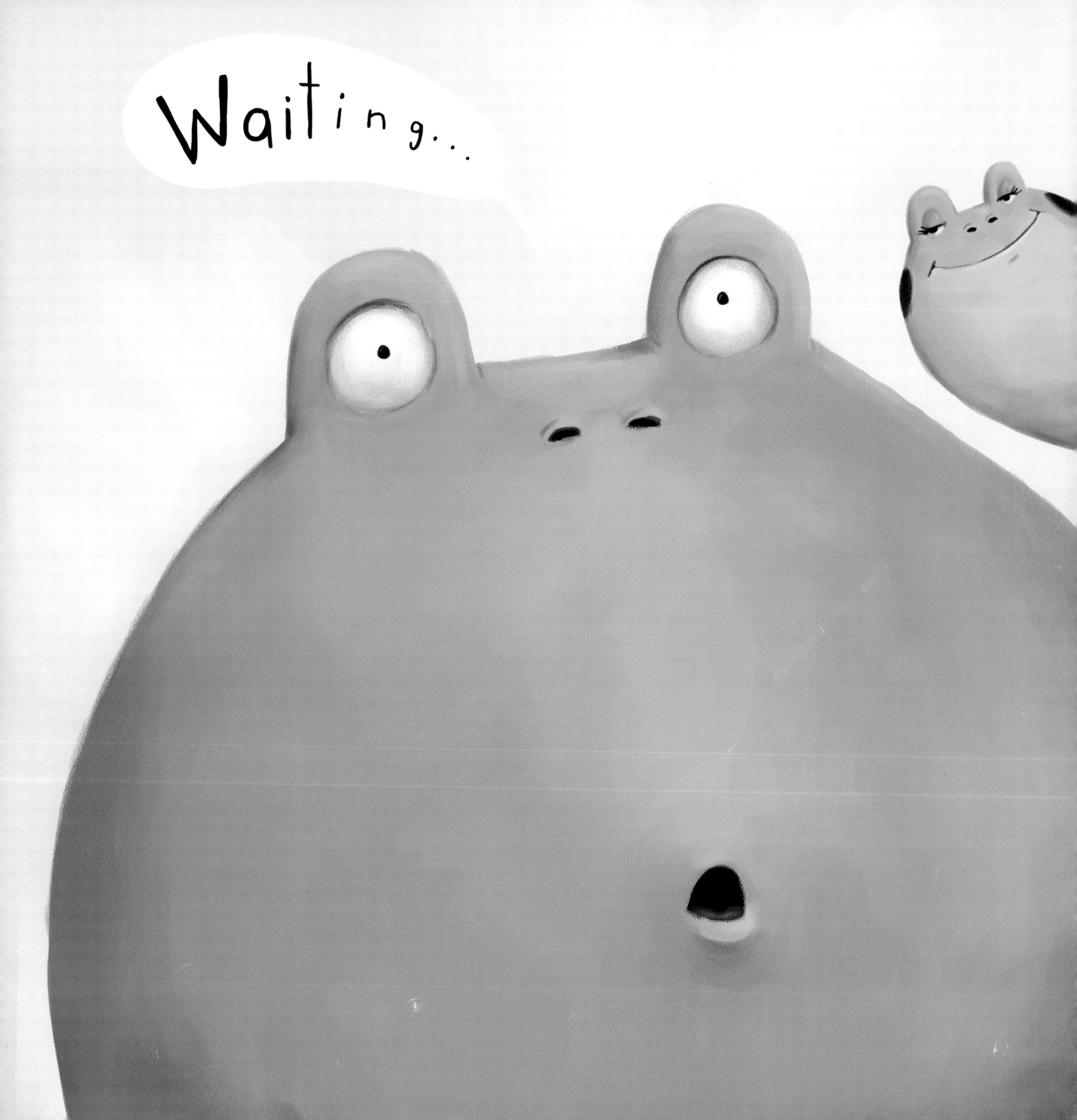
Waiting...

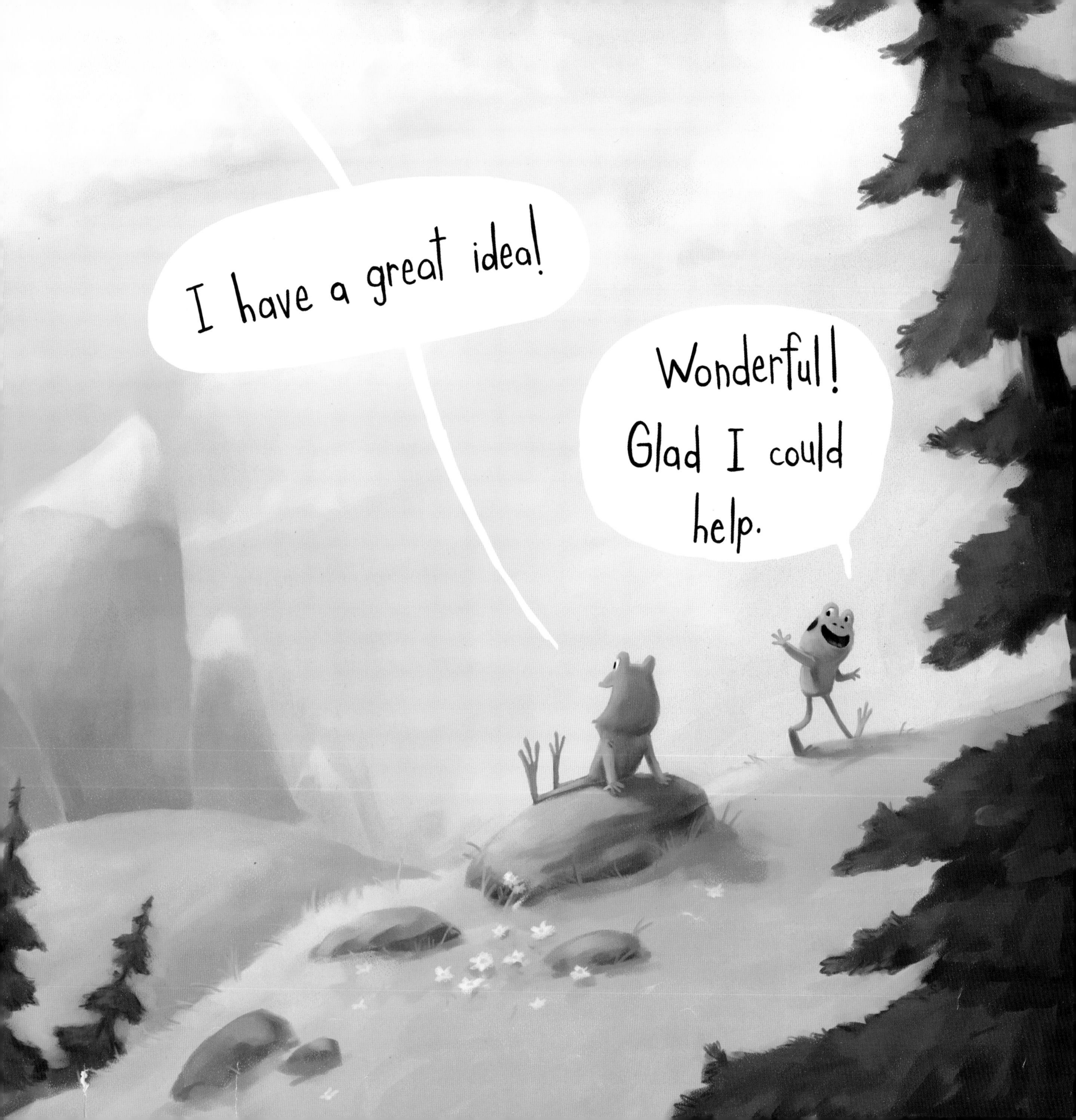
I have a great idea!
Wonderful! Glad I could help.

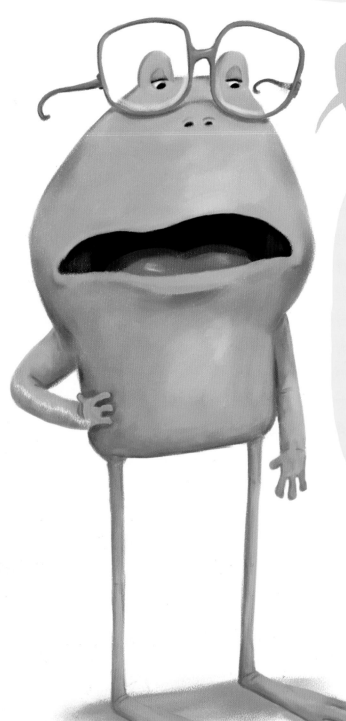

Sit with me for a minute.

So, what did you do all day?

Nothing. And you know what? It was **GREAT**. I came up with the **BEST** idea of what to do tomorrow.

I've got NOTHING to do!